Hello, Family Members,

Learning to read is one of the most important accomplishments of early childhood. **Hello Reader!** books are designed to help children become skilled readers who like to read. Beginning readers learn to read by remembering frequently used words like "the," "is," and "and"; by using phonics skills to decode new words; and by interpreting picture and text clues. These books provide both the stories children enjoy and the structure they need to read fluently and independently. Here are suggestions for helping your child *before*, *during*, and *after* reading:

Before

- Look at the cover and pictures and have your child predict what the story is about.
- Read the story to your child.
- Encourage your child to chime in with familiar words and phrases.
- Echo read with your child by reading a line first and having your child read it after you do.

During

- Have your child think about a word he or she does not recognize right away. Provide hints such as "Let's see if we know the sounds" and "Have we read other words like this one?"
- Encourage your child to use phonics skills to sound out new words.
- Provide the word for your child when more assistance is needed so that he or she does not struggle and the experience of reading with you is a positive one.
- Encourage your child to have fun by reading with a lot of expression . . . like an actor!

After

- Have your child keep lists of interesting and favorite words.
- Encourage your child to read the books over and over again. Have him or her read to brothers, sisters, grandparents, and even teddy bears. Repeated readings develop confidence in young readers.
- Talk about the stories. Ask and answer questions. Share ideas about the funniest and most interesting characters and events in the stories.

I do hope that you and your child enjoy this book.

> —Francie Alexander
> Reading Specialist,
> Scholastic's Learning Ventures

For Max,
a great fan of Hello Reader! books
— M.B. and G.B.

Special thanks to Laurie Roulston
of the Denver Museum of Natural History
for her expertise

Text copyright © 2001 by Melvin & Gilda Berger.

Photography credits:

Cover: Kim Heacox/Peter Arnold, Inc.; page 1: Dynamic Graphics; page 3: Stone; pages 4-5: Mark Carwardine/Still Pictures/Peter Arnold, Inc.; pages 6-7: BIOS/Y. Lefevre/Peter Arnold, Inc.; page 8: Auscape /J-M LaRoque/Peter Arnold, Inc.; page 9: Kelvin Aitken/Peter Arnold, Inc.; page 10: George D. Lepp/Photo Researchers, Inc.; page 11: John Hyde/Bruce Coleman Inc.; page 12: François Gohier/Photo Researchers, Inc.; page 13: Art Wolfe/Photo Researchers, Inc.; pages 14-15: D. Perrine/Peter Arnold, Inc.; page 16: Michel Jozon/Innerspace Visions; page 17: Michael S. Nolan/Innerspace Visions; page 18 (top): Doug Perrine/Innerspace Visions; page 18 (bottom): Norbert Wu; page 20: Fred Bruemmer/Peter Arnold, Inc.; page 21: Windland Rice/Bruce Coleman Inc.; page 22: Doug Perrine/Peter Arnold, Inc.; page 23: Horst Schafer/Peter Arnold, Inc.; page 24: DiMaggio/Kalish/Peter Arnold, Inc.; page 25: Mike Couffer/Bruce Coleman, Inc.; pages 26-27: François Gohier/Photo Researchers, Inc.; page 28: Doc White/Innerspace Visions; page 29: Ingrid Visser/Innerspace Visions; page 31: Stuart Westmorland/Stone; pages 32-33: François Gohier/Photo Researchers, Inc.; page 34: Tom Brakefield/Bruce Coleman Inc.; page 35: Oswaldo Vasquez/Innerspace Visions; page 37: Marilyn Kazmers/Innerspace Visions; page 39: AP/Wide World Photos, Inc.; page 40: Ingrid Visser/Innerspace Visions.

Library of Congress Cataloging-in-Publication Data

Berger, Melvin.
    Splash! : a book about whales and dolphins / by Melvin and Gilda Berger.
        p. cm. — (Hello reader! Science—Level 3)
    ISBN: 0-439-20166-7 (pbk.)
        1. Cetacea—Juvenile literature. [1. Whales. 2. Dolphins. 3. Cetaceans.] I. Berger, Gilda.
    II. Title. III. Hello science reader! Level 3.

QL737.C4 B65 2001
599.5—dc21   00-030807

10 9 8 7 6 5 4 3 2 1   01 02 03 04 05

Printed in the U.S.A.
First printing, May 2001

23

Splash!

A Book About Whales and Dolphins

by Melvin & Gilda Berger

Hello Reader! Science — Level 3

SCHOLASTIC INC.

Cartwheel ·B·O·O·K·S·®

New York Toronto London Auckland Sydney
Mexico City New Delhi Hong Kong

CHAPTER 1
As Big as Big Can Be

All whales are big.

But the blue whale is the BIGGEST.

- It's as high as a two-story building!
- It's as long as three buses!
- It's as heavy as twenty-five elephants!

The blue whale is the biggest animal
that ever lived.
It is even bigger than *Tyrannosaurus rex*!

Dolphins belong to the same family as whales.
But most dolphins are not as big as
most whales.

Whales look like fish.
But they're not fish.
Whales are mammals
- like dogs and cats,
- like cows and horses,
- and like you.

Like other mammals,
a baby whale is born alive.
It is born in shallow water,
tail first.

It may weigh
as much as 4,000
pounds at birth.
A baby whale is
called a calf.

At first the calf rolls
in the water like a barrel.
But the mother quickly turns it right side up.
Other whales help her push it to the surface.
And the calf takes its first breath of air.

The newborn calf feeds, or nurses,
from its mother's nipple.
The nipple squirts rich milk
into the baby's mouth.

The young calf nurses about 40 times a day.
Every day, it guzzles about 130 gallons
of milk.
And every day it gains about 200 pounds!
Soon the calf is ready to find its own food.

A whale is warm-blooded.

That means it stays warm, no matter
how cold the water.

Two heavy layers cover its body
like a blanket.

The top layer is the whale's skin.

It can be more than one foot thick!

Underneath is a layer of fat.

It is called blubber.

The blubber can be two feet thick!

You may know that a whale breathes air.
But it does not have a nose like yours.
Instead, a whale breathes through
an opening called a blowhole.
The blowhole is on top of the whale's head.
This lets the whale breathe while most
of its body stays underwater.

When a whale dives, it holds its breath.
One breath goes a long way.
Some whales can hold their breath
for up to two hours.
Try holding your breath.
One minute is tops!

Sooner or later, a whale must breathe.
Up it swims to the surface.
It breathes out the air in its lungs.

One day, you may see a whale
breathe out.
The air mixes with water.
It makes a cloud called a blow.

Not all blows are alike.
Some go straight up.
They can reach as high as a three-story
building.
Others spread out in a spray.
They look like a fountain against the sky.

You can see some blows for miles.
You can hear them for hundreds of feet.
And if you're close, you can smell them.
Most whales have very bad breath!

Deep ocean water is dark and murky.
It is hard for whales to see very far.
But sound travels very well through water.
So whales depend more on hearing
than on sight.

Whales have ears,
but the ears are hard to spot.
They are two tiny holes in the skin.
Yet, whales hear better than most people.

Whales can hear the different sounds
that other whales make.
They can hear one another miles apart.
The sounds help them keep in touch.

Sounds help whales in another way.
They let whales find objects underwater.
The whale makes the sounds.
Then it listens for the echoes that bounce back.

Some echoes come back quickly.
That means the object is close.
Some echoes take longer to return.
That means the object is far away.
Using sound to find things is called
echolocation (ek-oh-loh-KAY-shun).

CHAPTER 2
Whales With Teeth

Most whales have teeth.
They are called **toothed whales**.
The teeth are for catching prey.
They are not for chewing.
Toothed whales swallow their food whole
and alive.

The **sperm whale** is the biggest toothed whale.
It's a huge animal in many ways. It has
- the biggest head of any whale,
- the largest brain,
- the thickest skin,
- and the heaviest layer of blubber.

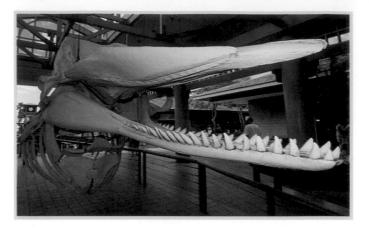

Fifty giant teeth line the sperm whale's lower jaw.

Each is several inches long.

And each weighs half a pound.

The sperm whale eats many kinds of fish.

But its favorite food looks like an octopus.

It is called a **squid**.

Instead of eight arms, a squid has ten arm

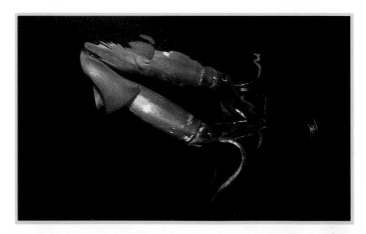

Squid come in all sizes.

Some are as small as cucumbers.

Others are as big as canoes.

The biggest ones are called **giant squid**.

Sperm whales hunt giant squid.

The squid live at the bottom of the sea.

Sperm whales dive very deep
to catch them.

Down a sperm whale drops
like a sleek submarine.

After about a mile, it nears the ocean floor.

It uses echolocation to find its prey.

A sperm whale can't always catch
a giant squid.

But when it does, the squid fights back.

The whale and squid battle it out.

But the whale usually wins.

It swallows the huge creature.

Narwhals are much smaller than sperm whales.

Most have only two teeth.

In male narwhals, one tooth sticks straight out.

It is eight feet long and comes to a sharp point.

The tooth is called a tusk.

No one knows why narwhals have tusks. Are they used

- to spear large fish?
- to dig shellfish out of the mud on the ocean bottom?
- to attract females?

The answer is a mystery.

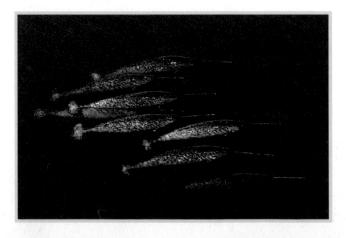

CHAPTER 3
Dolphins

Dolphins are small, toothed whales.
They are the biggest group of whales
with teeth.

Sailors tell about dolphins saving people.
Some years ago, a woman fell out
of her boat.
Three dolphins swam over.
They held her up in the water.
And they pushed her onto a beach.

Dolphins help each other in the same way.
Let's say one dolphin in a group is sick
or hurt.
The others carry it through the water.
They lift it to the surface to breathe.
They protect it against enemies.

Dolphins are playful.
They leap and turn in the water.
The young rub up against each other.
They play underwater tag.

People like to hear dolphins "talk."
Each bark, squeal, squawk, or whistle
seems to mean something different.
Scientists listen carefully to these sounds.
They try to discover the meanings.

You may know **bottle-nose dolphins** best.
Often you see them in water parks
and aquariums.
Their beaks make them look smiling
and happy.

Bottle-noses seem to be very smart.
Trainers can teach them to play basketball
or to jump through hoops.
One bottle-nose was the star of a TV show.

The **common dolphin** is smaller than
the bottle-nose.
It's also a better swimmer.

Common dolphins often swim
alongside ships.
They keep up with them, mile after mile.
From time to time, the dolphins leap
and flip in midair!

The biggest dolphin is the **orca**.
It mainly feeds on fish and squid.
But the orca also attacks other whales.
And it makes meals of penguins, seals,
and walruses.
No wonder some people call the orca
"killer whale."

Orcas hunt blue whales for their great
big tongues!

The tongue of a blue whale is an orca's
favorite food.

Orcas live in all the world's oceans.
Someday you may spot one
from far away.
You'll see a six-foot-high fin sticking up
from its back.
It's a sight you'll never forget!

CHAPTER 4
Toothless Wonders

The largest whales have no teeth.
Instead, hundreds of fuzzy plates hang down
from their upper jaws.
The plates are called **baleen** (buh-LEEN).
They look and feel like giant fingernails.
And they act like oversize strainers.

The **blue whale** is the largest baleen whale.
As it swims, it opens its gigantic mouth
very wide.
Tons of water flow right in.

The water holds millions of small, shrimplike creatures, or **krill**.

The whale closes its mouth.
Down come the baleen.
With its tongue, the whale squeezes
the water out through the baleen.
But the krill get stuck.
And the whale swallows its dinner.

The blue whale has an amazing appetite.
In one day, it gulps down about four tons
of krill!

The **humpback whale** is another baleen whale.
You may think the humpback whale has a hump on its back.
It does not.
The whale just humps, or shows its neck and back, when it dives!

Every now and then the humpback flip-flops in the air.
It is called breaching.
The whale suddenly leaps out of the water.
Its long, white flippers spread out like wings.
Then the humpback falls back into the water.
SPLASH!
The landing sounds like an exploding firecracker.

Humpback whales are the opera singers of the ocean.

Their "songs" last up to 20 minutes.

Each group of whales repeats its own song over and over again.

They never seem to get tired.

Right whales got their name long ago.
Whalers said they were the "right" ones
to hunt.
They were slow swimmers and easy
to catch.
And their bodies held lots of the oil
that the whalers wanted.

Long ago, many right whales swam
in the oceans.
But hunters killed them in great numbers.
Sad to say, few are left.

You can also tell a right whale
from far away.
Its blow is divided.
It looks like the letter V.

Sometimes right whales are
like sailboats.
Instead of sails, the whales raise
their tails in the air.
Their "sail-tails" catch the wind.
The wind pushes the whales from deep
to shallow water — and back again.

Right whales sometimes beat the water with their tails.

Or, they jump from the water and crash back with a mighty splash.

Sometimes one starts.

Then others follow.

Scientists wonder:

- Are the whales being playful?
- Are they keeping in touch with each other?
- Or are they looking for something good to eat?

CHAPTER 5
From Sea to Shining Sea

Whales live in all the oceans of the world.
Most swim in groups called pods.
Pods have from three to hundreds
of whales.

Some whales spend part of the year
in warm waters.
In summer, they migrate, or move.
They migrate to the cold waters
near the North and South poles.

Day and night, the pod swims slowly
through the water.
The trip may take several months.
The whales hardly stop to sleep or eat.
In case of trouble, they help each other.

The whales stay in the cold waters
for about three months.
The waters have lots of food.
Every day, the whales take in huge
amounts of krill and other sea creatures.
Their blubber gets very thick.

In time, the water begins to freeze.
The whales migrate back to warm water
before they get trapped by the ice.

Finally, they reach the warm waters.
Here the pregnant females give birth.
The mother whale stays close to her calf.
And she looks out for danger.

While in the warm waters, the whales stop eating.
They live off the fat of their blubber.

Soon it is summer again.
The whales gather in groups.
They start their long journey back to the cold waters.

From time to time, a whale swims
onto a beach.
The whale is said to be stranded.

The stranded whale must find its way back
into the sea.
Out of the water, whales find it hard
to breathe.

Sometimes other whales hear the cries
of a stranded whale.
They come to its aid.
Then they become stranded, too.

Stranded whales often live for several days.
They may even get back into the water.
Many times, people help.
If not, the stranded whales die.

Not long ago, a young whale was stranded.
The U.S. Coast Guard found it.

They named it Humphrey.

The sailors towed Humphrey

into shallow water.

Doctors examined the whale.

They found many germs in its blowhole.

So they gave the whale medicine.

In ten days, Humphrey was ready
to swim out to sea.
Boats and swimmers helped the whale
swim safely away.

One day you may find a stranded whale.
Call for help.
While waiting, keep away from the whale.
Then maybe your whale will live happily
ever after — just like Humphrey!